CANTERLOT HIGH STORIES

Pinkie Pie
and the Cupcake
Calamity

Arden Hayes

LITTLE, BROWN AND COMPANY

New York ♞ Boston

Little, Brown and Company
Hachette Book Group
1290 Avenue of the Americas, New York, NY 10104
Visit us at LBYR.com
MLPEG.com

First Edition: October 2018

Little, Brown and Company is a division of Hachette Book Group, Inc.
The Little, Brown name and logo are trademarks of Hachette Book Group, Inc.

The publisher is not responsible for websites (or their content)
that are not owned by the publisher.

Library of Congress Control Number 2018941024

ISBNs: 978-0-316-41342-8 (paper over board), 978-0-316-41340-4 (ebook)

Printed in the United States of America

LSC-C

10 9 8 7 6 5 4 3 2 1

CONTENTS

GIRLS RULE

CHAPTER
1

Cupcakes and Cheer

"Two huckleberry croissants, ready to go!" Pinkie Pie called out as she set them on the counter.

"We ordered two hot chocolates, too…" a woman with neon-green glasses said. She peeked over Pinkie's shoulder, looking for the mugs.

"Of course—I never forget!" Pinkie called out. "Our hot chocolates just take a little longer because they're made with real chocolate...and kindness and love and all the other good stuff that takes time."

Pinkie Pie offered the customer her sweetest just-one-more-minute smile and turned back to the stove. She stirred the melting chocolate pieces around and around until they were smooth enough to add to the milk. She was pretty quick to get up people's orders, but hot chocolate always slowed her down. Everything at Sugarcube Corner was done by hand and made to order just for the customer. It was what made the bakery so special. You could taste all the extra love and effort put into each one of their cakes and pies. It just wasn't always as quick as some people would've liked.

Pinkie Pie mixed the steamed milk and melted chocolate and poured it into two of her favorite mugs. One was painted with butterflies, and the other had tiny cherries all over it. She'd invited her friends to the café one afternoon so they could each paint a few mugs and plates for the owners of Sugarcube Corner, Mr. and Mrs. Cake, who had wanted the dishes to have that one-of-a-kind feel. They had to toss a few of the ones Rainbow Dash had made (she was more of an... *abstract artist*), but otherwise they'd turned out beautifully.

"Two hot chocolates with extra marshmallows," Pinkie Pie repeated to herself as she grabbed two miniature cookies and put them on the side of the saucers. She strode over to the woman's table and set them down in front of her and her young son. "And I threw in two chocolate chip cookies for dipping! You've had chocolate chip cookies before, but not like this. This is a special Sugarcube Corner recipe."

The woman bit into a cookie, and her eyes went wide. "These are delicious. What's in them?"

"It's a special *secret* Sugarcube Corner recipe," Pinkie Pie answered.

When Pinkie Pie turned back to the counter, she couldn't help smiling. It really didn't matter that the hot chocolate was a minute late; what mattered was that she cared about every single person who came into the café. Mr. and Mrs. Cake had taught her that. They loved treating their customers as if they were friends and family who had come to their home.

4

"We'll take one of everything!" called out a familiar voice.

Pinkie turned to see Twilight Sparkle standing in the front entrance. Rainbow Dash, Rarity, Applejack, Sunset Shimmer, and Fluttershy were at one of the sidewalk tables outside. They waved at Pinkie Pie through the window.

"Just kidding," Twilight said, bounding over. "But we *are* going to order some snacks."

She leaned on the counter, watching as Pinkie Pie grabbed a few stray dishes from an empty table and dropped them in the sink.

"The usual?" Pinkie Pie asked. Lately when her friends came in after school, they ordered a whole key lime pie, and each had a piece. Whenever she could, Pinkie Pie would take a five-minute break to eat with them.

"I think we're going to mix it up today," Twilight said. "Maybe a banana split pie? Or...is there anything else you think is spectacular?"

Twilight Sparkle's eyes lit up as she spoke. Pinkie Pie loved how much Twilight loved sweets. She was Sugarcube Corner's perfect customer, always wanting to try the latest red velvet cupcake or pumpkin walnut cookie.

Pinkie Pie smiled mischievously and waved her into the back room. "Follow me!"

The bakery was in the back of the shop, tucked behind the counter. It had a few long worktables and two huge refrigerators that stored all the cakes, pies, and cupcakes. Pinkie Pie went to the fridge and grabbed a freshly frosted cupcake off the shelf, along with a bowl of chocolate batter.

"This is our yummy cherry-cheesecake cupcake," she said, passing it to Twilight proudly. "Technically, they go on sale tomorrow, but I think I can sneak our best customers an early preview."

"Oh…*yummmm*…" Twilight Sparkle said through her first bite. "What's in the middle?"

"That's sweet cream," Pinkie explained. "Good, right? But not nearly as good as my mocha cocoa cupcake will be. I've been working on the recipe for weeks."

She dipped a spoon into the bowl and gave the batter to Twilight. Twilight took a taste and smiled. "It *is* good!"

"Right now it's good," Pinkie Pie said, "but by the time I perfect the recipe it'll be the most extraordinary cupcake you've ever tasted. I'm even thinking about making special toasted, roasted marshmallow frosting. *Mmmmm!*"

"Sounds delicious," Twilight said. "For now, we'll have to settle for a half-dozen delicious cherry-cheesecake cupcakes."

"Just a half dozen?" Pinkie Pie knew Twilight never could eat just one.

"Fine!" Twilight laughed. "Let's just get a whole dozen, and we'll bring some home."

"That's more like it," Pinkie Pie said as she pulled the tray from the refrigerator. "I'll bring them out to you."

Twilight returned to the front, and Pinkie Pie moved quickly around the kitchen, hand-frosting each cupcake. Then she made special designs on the top, using the tiniest piping bag she could find. A flower with

rainbow petals for Rainbow Dash, a purple lilac for Twilight Sparkle, an apple for Apple-jack, a bow for Rarity, a guitar for Sunset Shimmer, and a butterfly for Fluttershy. Brimming with pride when she was done, she stared down at her creations.

"These are perfect," said Pinkie Pie, assembling them on a tray.

And they were.

CHAPTER 2

A Little Help from Friends

"Geez!" Mr. Cake said as he carried a stack of plates into the kitchen. "This is the busiest Saturday we've had in a while."

Pinkie was at the stove, making six hot chocolates, while Mrs. Cake ran the register. Apparently, there had been a huge track meet at Canterlot High that morning, and now the whole team was at the café, along with their parents and friends. Pinkie Pie barely noticed when Rarity and Rainbow Dash came in.

"Do we really have to wait in this line?" Rainbow Dash said, half joking as they leaned against the counter. "It's practically out the door!"

"I know," Pinkie Pie said. "We weren't expecting a crowd today. But I guess the track team knows where to get the best cupcakes and cookies in town!"

"I'll need three peanut butter cookies and a dozen lemon cream cupcakes to go," Mrs. Cake called out from the register. She was talking to Pinkie Pie, of course, who was already elbow-deep in making hot chocolates. Pinkie wondered for a moment how she'd ever catch up to all these orders, but she knew she would. As Sugarcube Corner's best—and only—employee, she always did.

"Just one minute!" Pinkie called back, stirring the chocolate in an attempt to make it melt faster. Mr. Cake was running around the café, clearing tables and talking to customers. Pinkie desperately looked around for another set of helping hands, but there were only the three of them. They'd been working that way for years.

"We can help," Rainbow Dash said, noticing her friend's increasingly frantic expression. "What do you need?"

Pinkie Pie glanced over at Mrs. Cake, who shrugged her approval. "I mean, they're here every day," Mrs. Cake said. "They know the place better than most people. We could use some extra hands for a bit—"

"Great! Could you keep stirring this so it doesn't burn?" Pinkie Pie immediately asked Rainbow Dash. Then she pointed to the pitcher of steamed milk on the counter. "When it's fully melted, stir the milk into the pot. Then pour out six hot chocolates into those mugs. Rarity, you can come with me!"

Rainbow Dash raced behind the front counter and went to work, pulling down six different mugs. "Where are the ones I painted?" she asked herself quietly.

Pinkie Pie waved for Rarity to follow her into the back room. "We can frost the cupcakes really quickly," she said. "And the cookies are already done; we just have to throw them into a bag. Here!"

She pulled the tray of lemon cupcakes and a bowl of frosting from the fridge and set them down on the long table. Then she handed Rarity a spatula.

"What do I do?" Rarity asked, staring from the spatula to the cupcakes.

"Just smooth a little bit of frosting onto each one," Pinkie Pie explained. "Then, if you're feeling creative, you can make a flower or a bow or a heart. Those are the piping bags we use for decorating cakes and stuff. No pressure, though! Oh—and this is where the boxes are. For when they're done."

Pinkie Pie pointed around the room at

the different supplies. Then she grabbed more peanut butter cookies from the tray and brought them to Mrs. Cake. She put three in a bag and set them aside for the customer.

"Rarity's frosting the lemon cupcakes," she called to Mrs. Cake. "They'll be right out!"

"It shouldn't be long!" Mrs. Cake repeated to the customer, a blue-haired girl Pinkie Pie recognized from her gym class.

By the time Pinkie Pie had done this, Rainbow Dash had already served the customers their hot chocolates. Seeing there was still work to be done, she began busing tables. She set some empty mugs in the sink and refilled a napkin dispenser while Pinkie started washing some of the dirty dishes.

Mr. Cake ran around behind the counter, putting cookies and slices of pie onto different plates. "We need two slices of cookies-and-cream crumble at table fourteen," he said as he pointed to two girls from the track team.

Pinkie Pie dried two plates and put a fresh piece of pie on each. Then she ran the order over to the girls and sprinted back. She made sure to grab a few dirty mugs along the way. When she got to the counter, Rarity was there with the box of lemon cupcakes.

"Let's see," Pinkie Pie said, opening the top. "Wow!"

There were a dozen perfectly frosted cupcakes inside. Rarity's talent for design and sewing had somehow translated to cake decoration. She had made tiny yellow lemons on the top of each cupcake, complete with little stems and leaves. She just shrugged as if it were the easiest thing ever. "Darling, it was nothing compared to pulling together the diamond-encrusted line of Blitzball uniforms I made last semester."

"Wow is right," Mr. Cake said, peering into the box. "You're a natural!"

Even Mrs. Cake had taken a break from the register to look. "You know, we *could* use some extra help in the kitchen…" she said.

"Would you ever be interested in taking on a couple of shifts?" Mr. Cake asked. "Pinkie Pie could use help in the back, frosting cakes and organizing supplies. And we could teach you to run the register when it gets really busy."

Rarity looked surprised. "I suppose that could be kind of—"

"Fun!" Pinkie Pie finished her sentence. "*So* much fun! We'd be working together. Palling around, being pals at work and pals at school and pals at—"

"Yes, officially, yes." Rarity smiled, and Pinkie gave her a jumping squeeze.

Mrs. Cake grabbed one of the extra aprons from under the register and handed it to Rarity. "I'm glad. Consider today your first day. You're hired!"

Rarity and Pinkie Pie clasped hands. Pinkie Pie was so excited that she felt as if she might burst from happiness. Sure, working at Sugarcube Corner was fun, but it would be ten times more fun with Rarity working beside her. The pair darted into the back to make more cookies, hardly noticing Rainbow Dash walking over with a tower of dirty dishes. She seemed a little annoyed she hadn't been offered a shift, too.

"What am I…?" she said to no one in particular. "Minced meat?!"

CHAPTER

3

The Trouble with Rarity

Pinkie Pie looked at the clock for the tenth time. It was 3:22. 3:22! Which meant that Sugarcube Corner's newest employee, Rarity, was officially twenty-two minutes late.

"Where's Rarity?" Mrs. Cake asked. They'd just gotten a new shipment of supplies, and she was helping Mr. Cake unload it into the back of the café. She had come out to the register to drop off a brand-new box of melting chocolate.

"Um…she must be running late," Pinkie Pie said sheepishly. She hoped her friend wouldn't let down the Cakes.

"Hope everything's all right." Mrs. Cake gave her a sad smile before disappearing back into the kitchen.

Pinkie Pie grabbed one of the rags and started wiping down the counter. She wiped faster and faster, putting all her might into it. This was only Rarity's fourth shift at Sugarcube Corner, and already she was super late. Pinkie Pie had texted her once, but she hadn't heard anything back. Didn't Rarity realize how worried she was making Pinkie? She kept picturing Rarity in the middle of the street, a car screeching toward her. Or sick in bed and unable to get to the phone. Sure, Pinkie Pie had just seen her at school two hours ago, but what if something happened *after* school? Something terrible?

"Could I please have another piece of that pecan pie, Pinkie?" Feathers Grey looked up from his book. He was a silver-haired man who spent every afternoon in Sugarcube Corner, usually reading a new book. He always wore a green three-piece suit. Pinkie got the feeling he didn't have many people to talk to, so she made a point of being extra kind to him. She had to give him credit; he didn't seem to mind the packs of rowdy Canterlot High students who came by once school let out. He was always happily focused on whatever book he had brought to read that day.

"Of course, coming right up," Pinkie said. She went to the fridge in the back and cut him another slice, then arranged it on a pretty green plate with polka dots. She set it down in front of him just as Rarity walked in.

"You're okay!" Pinkie cried, running toward her and enveloping her friend in a massive hug. She let out a huge sigh of relief. "I was so worried!"

Rarity looked confused as she wiggled out of Pinkie's arms. "Darling, I'm *so* sorry I'm late. Did I worry you? I was just with Twilight Sparkle. You wouldn't believe it, but the strap on her shoe broke on her way to an after-school debate meet. Completely unwearable. So we had to stop by the Blooming Rose,

that new boutique on Main Street. I found these incredible boots for her. Lavender with sparkly laces. They're really quite fabulous. Totally pulled her look together, for the debate, too."

She breezed past Pinkie and grabbed her apron. Pinkie Pie took a deep breath and tried to smile. She knew Rarity had just been trying to help Twilight Sparkle, and of course no one appreciated a fabulous pair of shoes more than Rarity did. But couldn't she have responded to Pinkie's text or let Pinkie know she was going to be late? Pinkie really didn't want to be too harsh toward her friend, but Sugarcube Corner was so important to her and the Cakes, and they needed to be able to rely on Rarity.

"Oh…heh-heh….yeah, they sound real cool." Pinkie Pie tried her hardest to seem normal. "I was just worried…because you were supposed to be here at three." Pinkie added a grin to soften her nudging tone. She wasn't sure it was working.

"Oh, darling. I really am so sorry. I completely lost track of the time," Rarity said. "We went by that huge space two doors down. The one that's under construction? They still have paper in the windows, but I think it might be turning into a D-Light Shoe Outlet. Wouldn't that be spectacular?"

"Yeah, totally." Pinkie organized the table with the sugars and creamers. Now that Rarity was here, Pinkie would just try to have a good shift with her. It didn't matter that Rarity dropped a whole sack of sugar yesterday or that she forgot to wipe down the counters after her shift.

Mrs. Cake popped her head out of the back.

"Oh, Rarity, you're finally here," she said. Pinkie couldn't tell if she was mad, because Mrs. Cake was usually in a pretty good mood. "The kitchen's a mess right now. Boxes everywhere. Maybe you could work the counter with Pinkie while we clean up."

"That's great!" Rarity said. She finished up a few texts on her phone before tucking it into the front of her apron. "I love working the register."

Pinkie gave her biggest, brightest fake smile. In the whole time she'd worked at Sugarcube Corner, she'd used her phone *maybe* twice (and once was today to check on Rarity). The whole point of working a shift was that you were supposed to *work*! Not text on your phone!

She was just about to say something to Rarity when Feathers Grey came up to the counter. He pulled his wallet from his coat pocket.

"Just wanted to settle up for the slices of pie," he said, counting out a few bills.

"How's that book you're reading? It looks super interesting, Feathers!" Pinkie rang up his order on the register. Then she took the bills and made change for him, dropping a few coins into his hand.

"Oh, very good. It's about this lion tamer who..." He paused, noticing Rarity staring at him. Her hand was placed thoughtfully on her chin. She'd actually walked around the side of the counter to see his whole outfit. "Um…is something the matter?" he asked.

"No, no, all wrong," Rarity said, pointing up and down at his three-piece suit. "You're going to want to do blues, purples. Green doesn't work as well with your skin tone."

"Oh! Ha, *umm*, ha-ha. Rarity, you silly goose! Don't mind her, Feathers." Pinkie Pie ran out from behind the counter and got right between them, ushering Feathers to the door. She whispered under her breath, "She's just *teasing*. I love green on you.…It goes perfectly with your…uh… book!" She pointed down at the book in his hand, which had a dark-green cover.

"Oh, thanks," Feathers said as he left. "Yeah, I always thought it was nice, but maybe not. Anyway…see you tomorrow."

As soon as Pinkie was sure he was gone, she whipped around and gave Rarity her most serious "please tell me that was a dream and didn't actually happen" look.

"What?" Rarity just shrugged. "Did I say something wrong?"

CHAPTER 4

A New Neighbor

The next day, Pinkie Pie was working behind the counter when a woman with big blue-and-pink-striped hair walked in. She was checking her watch as she spoke. Then she glanced over her shoulder, looking for the room's different exits.

"I have an order under the name Amber

Glow," she said. "I called it in a few days ago. If you don't mind, I'm in a bit of a rush."

She glanced around the café, tapping her foot as though she couldn't wait to get out of there. Then she let out a long, annoyed sigh.

"Yes, of course." Pinkie smiled. "One pickup order coming right up! Let me just go grab it."

Pinkie slipped into the back room. Rarity was there, rubbing at a spot on her skirt. There were a few dozen cupcakes on the table and some piping bags scattered about. Pinkie ran over to the shelf where all the pickup orders usually were, but there was only a box for someone named Blackberry Soda.

"Ugh!" Rarity said, wiping carefully at her skirt. "This frosting is so hard to get out once it dries. I shouldn't have worn

tulle. I should probably invest in an apron that matches the decor in here....Hmm..." Rarity eyed the wallpaper for inspiration.

"Rarity, where's the order for Amber Glow?" Pinkie asked. "It was for three dozen cupcakes. I think it was for pickup today at noon?"

Pinkie went to the fridge and checked in there, but nothing. They weren't on any of the shelves in the back, either.

"Amber Glow?" Rarity stared off into the distance as if the name sounded familiar, but she couldn't remember why. "*Hmmm... Amber...Glow...*"

"Yes! Do you remember now?" Pinkie Pie got excited. Maybe this mix-up wasn't so bad. "Do you remember filling the order? I think it was a dozen peanut-butter-filled cupcakes, another dozen red velvet ones—"

"Wait…no…" Rarity dotted her skirt with the towel. "I thought those were for tomorrow." Rarity looked up at Pinkie with apologetic eyes, realizing she'd likely made a mistake.

Just then, Pinkie Pie ran to the stack of papers on the frosting table, sifting through them. Amber's order was all the way at the bottom. Rarity completed five of the orders that were being picked up that day, but she'd somehow totally missed the date on Amber Glow's.

"Oh no…" Pinkie said, staring at the sheet. How were they going to frost thirty-six cupcakes in two minutes? And do everything else they were supposed to do in the café? Like help customers and make hot chocolate and clear the tables outside? It wasn't possible. They would need to have like a billion hands! "This might be really bad. Really, *really* bad."

"Did I get the date wrong? Oh, darling, I'm so, so sorry. I could've sworn they were for tomorrow…" Rarity said with concern in her voice. She followed Pinkie out of the back room.

Pinkie went to the counter to speak to Amber Glow. She tried her best, most apologetic smile, furrowing her eyebrows to show she really didn't want to say what she was about to say.

"I'm so sorry," Pinkie Pie started, putting on her cheeriest voice. "But there was a mix-up with your order, and it won't be ready for another half hour. Is it possible for you to come back then?"

"*What?*" Amber Glow asked, as if she hadn't heard correctly.

"I'm really sorry," Pinkie repeated. "Your order—"

"It's definitely *not* possible for me to come back," Amber said, her voice somehow even more impatient than before. "I'm supposed to bring those cupcakes to a birthday party that starts in five minutes."

"Maybe we could deliver them," Pinkie tried. "If you tell us where—"

"That's okay," Amber said. "I'm going to see if the new Butter's Bakery has opened. I doubt something like this would happen there."

Before Pinkie Pie could say anything else, Amber Glow turned on her heel and left. Pinkie wanted to tell Rarity that this was terrible for business and she had to be super-careful about pickup orders, but

Pinkie was too worried about what the woman had just said.

"Butter's Bakery? Like the chain?" asked Rarity.

Pinkie ran to the window and peered outside. Amber went over to the two-story building where the construction had been happening. There weren't tables outside, but the paper had been taken off the windows. A man in yellow overalls was stenciling a sign on the glass: BUTTE.

" 'Butte.' That's actually kind of funny," Rarity said.

Pinkie ignored her, watching as Amber Glow paused at the door, then left when she realized it wasn't open yet. She had taken one of the to-go menus by the door. "Oh no," Pinkie said.

There were already five other Butter's Bakeries in town. They must churn out hundreds of coffees and hot chocolates a day, and thousands of cookies and pastries. Each Butter's Bakery was exactly the same as the others, with big yellow armchairs and mass-produced chalkboard signs. Pinkie was sure their treats were still delicious, but were they filled with happiness and love like Sugarcube Corner's were?

"If a Butter's Bakery opens right across the street, what's going to happen to Sugarcube Corner?" Rarity asked.

Pinkie Pie just stood there, staring at the half-painted sign. She didn't know the answer, but she had a feeling she didn't want to. How could they compete with a huge chain like Butter's Bakery?

They would have to try.

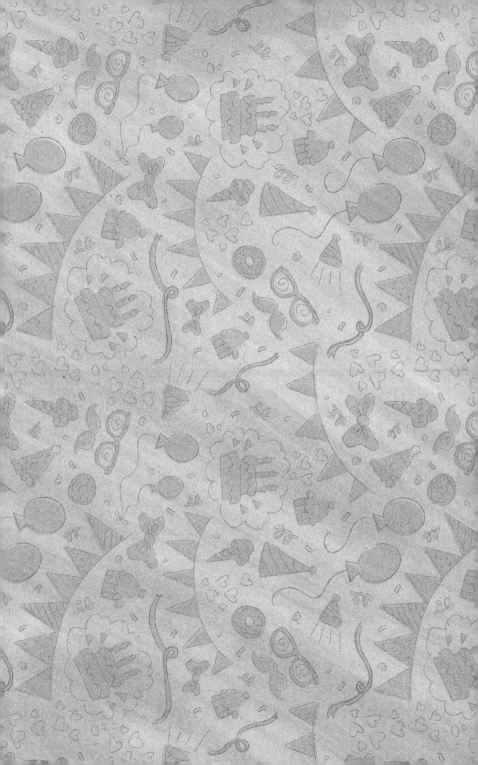

CHAPTER
5

See for Yourself

"This is not good," Mrs. Cake said. Butter's Bakery had opened only an hour ago, and they already had a line down the block. They were giving out free cookies to the first one hundred people who stopped by.

It had been two days since Amber Glow had told them about the new bakery, and

Pinkie Pie's stomach had been in knots the whole time. She'd been the one to break the news to Mr. and Mrs. Cake. It wasn't the easiest thing she'd ever done, but she didn't want them finding out by seeing the new sign in the window. Now they were all worried about what Butter's Bakery would mean for their little café.

"How are we going to compete with them?" Mr. Cake asked.

"We're Sugarcube Corner, that's how!" Pinkie Pie tried. She wanted to make them feel better, even if she didn't feel so great herself. "Everything you make is filled with love and warmth and ooey-gooey happiness. Butter's serves their drinks in paper cups, even if you're having them there. There's no love in that!"

"I bet their hot chocolate isn't as good as ours," Rarity added.

Pinkie Pie smiled at her friend. Since they'd heard the news, it was hard to be frustrated when Rarity made mistakes or walked in a little late. Everything seemed less important compared to their new competition across the street.

"Look, everyone still loves us." Pinkie Pie pointed around the café. A bunch of tables were full. Feathers Grey had come back, even after Rarity had insulted his suit, and he was reading at his favorite table in the corner. "You've been here for years. People aren't going to stop coming to Sugarcube Corner just because a Butter's Bakery opened!"

Mr. and Mrs. Cake smiled the tiniest bit.

"I hope you're right," Mr. Cake said. Then they both disappeared into the back room.

"I'm going to take my break," Pinkie Pie said. "Can you manage alone for fifteen minutes?"

Pinkie had a feeling she knew the answer to that. Rarity wasn't great at doing anything in the store on her own, but Pinkie really hoped her friend would step up when she had to. And Pinkie absolutely had to take her break now. She had important business to attend to.

"I'll be fine!" Rarity said as she put some fresh cookies in the glass case. She put the sugar cookies in front of a sign that said OATMEAL COOKIES, but Pinkie Pie just smiled widely and swapped them around when Rarity turned her back.

Pinkie grabbed sunglasses and an old

scarf from the Lost and Found box. Then she darted out the door, putting them on as she walked up the street. She didn't want people thinking Sugarcube Corner's best employee was going to Butter's Bakery for their mocha lattes or hazelnut muffins.

The truth was, she needed to see it for herself. Could Butter's Bakery really be great enough to steal Sugarcube Corner's business? She'd been into a Butter's only once before, and she didn't think it came anywhere close to Sugarcube Corner. That must've been five years ago, but still....

She slipped in the front door, past the line of people waiting for their free cookie. Inside it was...fine. Just fine! So totally normal. There were the same yellow chairs she remembered from the other Butter's Bakeries. They had some pastries in a fridge by

the register, but they looked rock hard—not nearly as soft and delicious as the ones at Sugarcube Corner. And the worst part was, it didn't seem like a place you'd want to spend a lot of time. It was crowded and loud, and there was music blasting from every speaker.

"Three hot coco-ramas ready to go!" an orange-haired boy behind the counter called out. A customer came by and picked up the cups.

Pinkie Pie stood there, staring at the boy as he made three more hot chocolates. He was using a huge, four-foot long machine. It took him less than a minute to fill up the other orders.

Pinkie's stomach dropped. She'd tried to be optimistic before, but it was hard to be now. Butter's Bakery was everything

Sugarcube Corner wasn't: fast and easy. They could serve a dozen customers in the time it took Pinkie to serve one. They probably shipped their cupcakes in from a factory that made thousands every hour.

"Can I help you with something?" the orange-haired boy asked, noticing Pinkie standing nearby. She suddenly remembered she was still wearing the sunglasses and scarf, even though she was inside.

"No, that's okay," she said dejectedly.

Then she took off down the street, back to Sugarcube Corner.

CHAPTER
6

Waiting for the Big Idea

Pinkie Pie wished she'd been wrong about Butter's Bakery, but she wasn't. It took only a week before things started to change at Sugarcube Corner. She and Rarity were working one Friday, which was usually their busiest night, but only a few people had come in. The usual crowds of Canterlot

High kids had decided to try out Butter's. Pinkie spotted them all at the sidewalk tables down the street.

"Are all the cupcakes frosted?" Pinkie Pie made her way through the kitchen, checking different shelves and cabinets. She'd already rearranged the supply drawers. "What about the pickup orders? Are those finished?"

"We only had two," Rarity answered, pointing to the stack of papers with her nail file before she returned to her manicure. "I double-checked, just to be sure. Everything's done."

Mr. and Mrs. Cake were working the front counter, so there wasn't much to do. Pinkie Pie had already wiped down all the tables, organized and reorganized the sugars and creamers, and baked a fresh batch of chocolate chip cookies. They were now sitting on a plate in the front of the bakery, just waiting for someone to eat them.

"I even made a new batch of frosting," said Rarity, glancing up from her nails and grabbing her phone. "Maybe our friends want to come by. That might cheer up the Cakes a little bit. I'll text them."

Normally, the idea of Rarity sitting in the back room, doing her nails and texting their friends, would have annoyed Pinkie Pie. But tonight she was grateful for her. Pinkie pulled some ingredients off the shelf and started mixing a new recipe for her mocha cupcake. It was the only thing that made her feel better lately. She'd started using a special chocolate that was much richer than the regular kind.

"Maybe it's just an off night..." Pinkie

said as she mixed a few cups of flour into the bowl. "Maybe once people start going to Butter's, they'll realize it's not so great after all."

"It really *isn't* that great," Rarity agreed. "But I don't know, Pinkie.... We haven't had many customers all week. I had to throw away two absolutely scrumptious pies last night because no one bought them."

Pinkie whipped the batter around with her spatula, then tasted it. The recipe was getting better, little by little, but she still hadn't gotten it quite right. She put in a few drops of vanilla and tasted it again. That was a tiny bit better.

"Did you see what happened yesterday?" Rarity asked, lowering her voice. "That group of seniors from Canterlot High came in, and then they turned around and left and went to Butter's. I could hardly look at Mr. Cake. I've never seen him so upset."

"I know. It was awful," Pinkie said with a sigh. The Cakes were always such cheerful people, but lately they were smiling less and less. Pinkie would turn around and hear them whispering to each other or sharing a worried look. Mrs. Cake had started counting the register at the end of the night. She was never in a good mood when she was done.

"Rarity! Pinkie Pie! Your friends are here!" Mr. Cake called into the back room.

Pinkie Pie left the cake batter and peered out front. Rainbow Dash, Sunset Shimmer, Twilight Sparkle, Fluttershy, and Applejack were all sitting at one of the big tables in the corner. They'd ordered a whole pie, a stack of cookies, and a round of hot chocolates.

Pinkie didn't think she'd ever been so happy to see them.

"These hot chocolates are incredible, Mr. Cake!" Twilight Sparkle called out. She held her mug in the air to toast him.

"The pie, too. Your pecan is my favorite," Applejack said between massive bites.

Pinkie Pie, Rarity, and the Cakes went over to their table. Pinkie used to be too busy to really hang out with her friends when they came in, but the place was so quiet now, she could've sat for a while.

Mrs. Cake was actually smiling as she watched Applejack inhale her pie. "I'm so glad you're enjoying it," she said. Then she let out a deep sigh. "That makes me happy. It's just...I'm not sure how much longer we're going to be around now that Butter's Bakery is right across the street."

"Don't say that," Fluttershy said. "The town just wouldn't be the same without Sugarcube Corner."

Mr. Cake nodded, but he didn't look at them. "It doesn't feel that way lately. I'm afraid we'll have to close if we keep having nights like this one."

He gestured to the empty café. Only two other people were there—Feathers Grey and a freshman who was studying for an exam. Rarity was right; it was so hard to see the Cakes sad. Pinkie Pie could hardly stand it.

"We'll just have to get creative!" Pinkie tried to cheer up Mr. Cake. "We can come up with some ideas so more Canterlot High students will come to the café, or maybe we could draw in a new crowd—senior citizens! Maybe Feathers Grey will bring his

friends." Pinkie sent a toothy grin in Feathers's direction.

Sunset Shimmer made a face. "I think most of Feather Grey's friends are—"

"We'll think of something, I promise," Pinkie Pie interrupted.

"Yeah, there has to be some way to drum up more business," Rarity agreed.

Mrs. Cake glanced sideways at Mr. Cake. She smiled sadly. "I hope so," she said. "We spoke about it, and we're going to give it a few more weeks. If things keep going the way they're going…"

"We'll figure something out," Pinkie Pie repeated. She didn't think she could bear hearing the rest of that sentence.

"You girls are some of the most creative kids we know." Mr. Cake nodded. "If anyone can do it, you can."

"Don't worry about a thing," Pinkie Pie went on. "There's no way I'll let anything happen to Sugarcube Corner."

Mrs. Cake gave Pinkie Pie the biggest, warmest hug, and then she and Mr. Cake both went back to the counter. It wasn't until they were out of earshot that Twilight Sparkle turned to Pinkie. "So…what's the plan?" she whispered.

Pinkie Pie looked around the empty café. She had so many good memories at Sugarcube Corner. Mr. and Mrs. Cake had given Pinkie her first job. Over the years she'd had birthday parties and Valentine's Day parties here. It was the place she and her friends always went to after dances or Blitzball games. She couldn't imagine this space being anything other than what it was.

"I don't know…" Pinkie admitted. "But

I will never give up, no matter what. I owe Mr. and Mrs. Cake that much."

"We're here to help," Twilight Sparkle added.

"I'll eat as much cake and pie as I can." Applejack shoveled another bite into her mouth. "Just doin' my part."

Pinkie Pie was happy to have her friends' help—she was. But first she had to come up with some spectacular ideas...and fast. She didn't have much time.

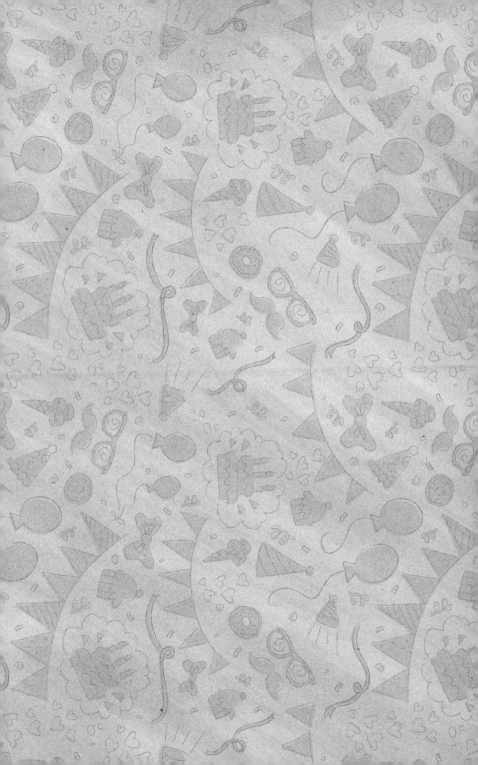

CHAPTER 7

A Sweet Mess

"Come in, come in!" Pinkie Pie said as she rushed from one customer to the next. "Find a seat next to the cake of your choice. Write out a name tag so you can make new friends! We'll begin shortly!"

Rarity and Twilight Sparkle brought out a few more cakes from the back, while

Fluttershy and Applejack put down bowls of frosting, piping bags, and different decorating tools. Each table was covered with a plastic cloth so customers could get as messy as they wanted. Rarity had even made little plastic smocks for everyone. *Sugarcube Corner* was written on the front of each.

In the corner, Rainbow Dash and Sunset Shimmer were on their guitars. They were supposed to be playing relaxing, quiet tunes, but Pinkie Pie could tell it was hard for them to control themselves. They both kept wanting to rock out and really show off their talents. Every now and then, the volume would spike and Pinkie Pie had to ask them to turn it down.

"Good work, Pinkie Pie!" Mrs. Cake said excitedly. She glanced around the packed room. Almost every seat was full. Each customer had a plain small cake in front of them, along with some tools and frosting. "I haven't seen the café this full in…well, ever."

"Let's hope it stays that way," Pinkie said. "If even half this crowd starts coming back, we should be okay. I want everyone to know what a fun, happy place Sugarcube Corner is, if they don't already."

"Well, they're going to have a lot of fun today. That's for sure!" Mrs. Cake laughed. She went over to greet two women she recognized from her knitting group. Pinkie Pie had come up with the plan to sell tickets to a cake decorating party, so Sugarcube Corner was making money *and* winning new customers, too.

"Ready?" Rarity asked. She signaled for Rainbow Dash and Sunset Shimmer to cut the music. "It's your time to shine…." She nudged Pinkie Pie up in front of the counter, where everyone could see her.

"Thank you all for coming to Sugar-cube Corner's first annual cake decorating party!" Pinkie said loudly. "Decorating cakes and cupcakes is one of my favorite things to do. It's fun and relaxing, and you get to use your creativity. Plus—there's so much sugar you can use! Today we're going to teach you a few easy tricks of the trade so you can make your very own dream cake. Just sit back, enjoy the music, and we'll be here to answer all your cake decorating questions! Wahoo!"

Rainbow Dash and Sunset Shimmer started the music again, and this time they really got into the groove. They played loudly but not too loudly, and soon people were bopping their heads and swaying in their seats as they frosted their cakes.

Rarity and Pinkie Pie went around to all the guests and showed them how to smoothly apply the frosting so crumbs didn't get stuck in it. Pinkie Pie gave the best directions she could to a woman named Root Beer, who was wearing a yellow polka-dotted dress. But Root Beer kept stabbing at the cake.

"What am I doing wrong?" Root Beer asked as a giant chunk of cake got mashed up in her frosting. "This is a mess."

Pinkie tried to fix it for her, but the cake still had a gaping hole in it.

"Maybe you can cover it with some flowers," Pinkie tried. She took the piping bag and made a few petals. "You do one petal at a time, like this. Just go around in a circle, squeezing out the same amount of frosting each time."

Pinkie made a tiny flower with pink frosting, and then she handed the bag to Root Beer. Root Beer grabbed it with both hands and shot a giant glob of frosting across the table. It hit her friend Holly Branch right in the nose.

"Gross," Holly Branch said, wiping at it before sneakily licking the frosting off her fingers.

Then Root Beer went right back to frosting the cake. She shot glob after giant glob of pink frosting onto it, until Pinkie couldn't even tell what was under it. Frosting dripped down the sides of the plate and onto the floor.

"This really doesn't look right," Root Beer kept saying.

Pinkie Pie glanced around the room. Rarity was helping a girl who'd given up on using the tools and had just started swirling the frosting with her finger. Another group of Canterlot High girls had started decorating one another's cakes. They drew silly faces and wrote their initials in messy script.

"This isn't going quite the way we planned," Rarity whispered as she passed Pinkie Pie. Their friends ran around cleaning up stray splatters of frosting that had landed on the wall. Fluttershy circled the room with paper towels, trying to keep the guests clean. Applejack was mopping up a particularly big pile of frosting, but the mop got so sticky it was making everything worse.

"It is a little... *messy*...." Pinkie let out a small laugh. She tried to stay positive for the rest of the party, but it seemed as if each creation was worse than the last. There were only two girls from Canterlot High who'd put any effort into their decorating, carefully making different designs on the tops of their cakes.

When it was time to go, the guests each picked up their plates. Some were still dripping. Pinkie Pie and Rarity had planned on putting each cake in a gorgeous bakery box, but they were so messy it seemed impossible now. Root Beer's cake was starting to fall apart.

"Thanks for everything!" Pinkie Pie called out as Root Beer and Holly Branch started up the street. "See you soon!"

Pinkie Pie watched them through the window. A group of people were coming down the street with shopping bags. They paused on the sidewalk, staring at the cakes in horror. A man with purple glasses asked them something Pinkie couldn't hear.

"We got them at Sugarcube Corner!" Holly Branch said cheerfully, pointing inside. Pinkie Pie's eyes went wide. She was so happy their customers were proud of their cakes! But this wasn't exactly great advertising for the bakery. Then Root Beer and Holly Branch walked away, leaving the crowd behind.

"Oh no! That's definitely not the reputation we want," Pinkie Pie said after she and Rarity had helped the other guests out.

"Maybe it didn't go precisely the way you planned," Rarity tried. "But the karaoke party will be better."

"I cannot wait!" Rainbow Dash had stopped playing and was packing up her guitar. "Next Saturday, right?"

"That's right," Pinkie Pie said proudly. "Karaoke Saturdays. A new Sugarcube Corner tradition!"

She glanced around the café, which looked as if a giant barrel of frosting had exploded in it. Fluttershy and Twilight Sparkle were picking bits of sugar out of each other's hair. Pinkie tried hard not to look at Mrs. Cake. Her face was frozen in a fake smile as she chipped away at some icing on the glass case.

Next week would be better. Pinkie Pie was sure of it.

It had to be!

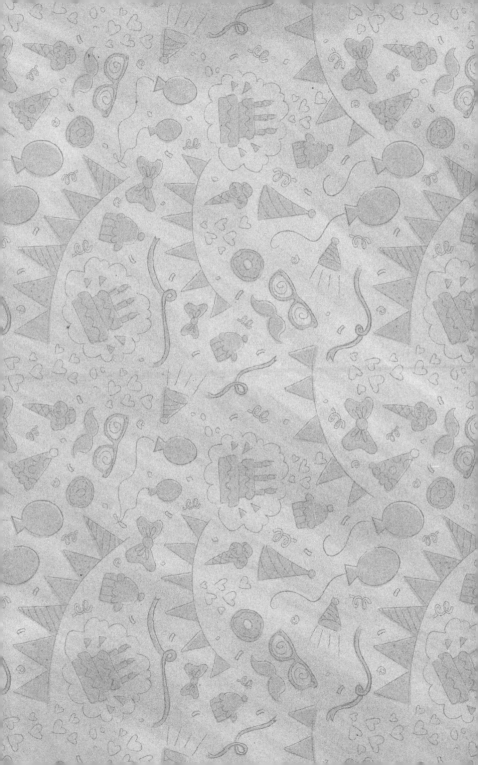

CHAPTER 8

Off Tune

The Sonic Rainbooms set up in the corner of the café, leaving room for a singer to move around and perform. Pinkie Pie took her place at the drums, Rarity was on the keytar, Fluttershy was on the tambourine, and Applejack was on the bass. Rainbow Dash was playing the guitar, but Twilight

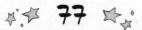

Sparkle and Sunset Shimmer had decided not to join so they could help the Cakes serve refreshments. The karaoke-ing hadn't even started yet, and they'd already sold out of cookies.

Pinkie Pie hit the hi-hats with her sticks, just to loosen up. Then she riffed a little on the snare drum. Rarity played some notes on her keytar as Rainbow Dash reached into the hat to draw out the first name. They'd passed it around before the show, to get volunteers to sing. Each name was written on a folded piece of paper, along with the song they wanted to perform.

"Thank you all for coming out tonight for Sugarcube Corner's first-ever karaoke night," Rainbow Dash said into the mic. "We're the Sonic Rainbooms, and we're going to be giving you live music for all your soulful serenading."

The audience clapped and cheered. Staring out into the dimly lit café, surrounded by her friends, Pinkie Pie felt her spirits lift. For the first time since the cake decorating party, she really felt they'd be okay. Sugarcube Corner and Mr. and Mrs. Cake would make it; she really wanted to believe that.

"First up is…" Rainbow Dash turned back, looking to Pinkie for the drumroll. Pinkie gave her a long, drawn-out one. "Blue Reeds! He'll be singing 'Lonely Hearts.'"

A tall, thin man with wild green hair stood up and came to the mic. Pinkie Pie suddenly got nervous. She felt as if he'd either be a really, really good singer or terrible. She'd been hoping they could at least begin the night with some great entertainment.

Pinkie Pie started in on the bass drum, remembering the notes for "Lonely Hearts." It was an old song, but she'd heard it a hundred times before. Blue Reeds took a deep breath, then belted out the most gorgeous line Pinkie Pie had ever heard.

"Sweet lonely heart of miiiiine," he sang. *"Always longing for the day when you'll be here with* meeeeeeee."

The audience exploded into applause. Mr. and Mrs. Cake stopped serving pie and just watched Blue Reeds sing the rest of the lines. He closed his eyes and leaned back as he sang, letting out the most powerful notes. Pinkie Pie thought he had to be a professional.

After he finished, Rainbow Dash called up a young girl named Melodies. Her name seemed like a good sign. But when they started the song "Clouds and Sunbeams," she wailed the lyrics into the mic. It was so loud and screechy that Pinkie Pie winced with every word.

They suffered through that song, and then the next one, which was sung by Feathers Grey. Pinkie really did consider him a friend, but Feathers couldn't stay in tune if his life depended on it. His voice cracked as he sang, and at one point he was so off-key that a table in the front walked out.

"Should *we* just play a few songs?" Applejack asked Pinkie Pie. "Give the crowd a break for a little bit? It seems like they could use some ... *on-key* music."

"But the hat is full of names...people came because they want to sing." Pinkie Pie pointed to the baseball cap. People kept coming up and dropping their names and requests into it. It was filled to the brim.

Rainbow Dash was about to draw another name when Twilight Sparkle came over to the band. She was holding a tray of dirty dishes. She leaned down and whispered in Pinkie Pie's ear. "I have some not-so-great news..." she said. "Butter's Bakery is having their jazz night tonight. It's kind of a big deal."

"Oh no..." Pinkie said. "No wonder we didn't get as big of a crowd as we wanted."

The audience was only half full, but Pinkie Pie had tried to be optimistic about it. A half-full café was a much bigger crowd than they were used to lately. She'd hoped more would come in off the sidewalk. There were always people walking by on Saturday nights.

"They have this whole jazz band there, and they turned on the fireplaces," Twilight continued.

"They have *fireplaces*?" Pinkie Pie asked as her heart started to sink. Out of all the things she'd heard about Butter's Bakery, this was the thing that scared her the most.

"I know, it's bad," Twilight said. "I just thought you should know...just so you didn't take it personally if some customers leave. I heard two boys saying they're going in a minute...."

"Right, yeah," Pinkie Pie said. "This is still going to be okay!"

Mr. and Mrs. Cake moved around the dimly lit café, dropping off mugs of coffee

and hot chocolate. Mrs. Cake gave Pinkie a big smile as she served a table a whole apple pie. Pinkie knew this was a much better crowd than they'd gotten all week, but karaoke was supposed to be their biggest night yet. How was that going to happen if everyone left soon? How could Sugarcube Corner compete with a fancy jazz band and fireplaces?

She nodded to Rainbow Dash, who plucked another name from the hat. The next person to sing, an older woman named Jamboree, was worse than the two others combined. As she shrieked and wailed, a dozen people left.

Pinkie Pie just kept playing the drums. She played with all her might, hoping her enthusiasm would help the crowd. But one by one, the tables cleared out, leaving only a few singers behind.

Come on, Pinkie, we need a plan, Pinkie thought as she listened to Feathers Grey perform a slow ballad about a missing cat. *I'm sure there's something else we can do....*

CHAPTER 9

One More Try

"How's that recipe coming?" Mrs. Cake asked, striding into the kitchen. Pinkie Pie was working away on her mocha cupcake, but it still wasn't where it needed to be. It needed to be the Best. Cupcake. *EVER*.

"I think I've finally made the perfect batter recipe," she said, holding up the tiny cake she'd baked that afternoon. "But I haven't quite figured out the cream stuffing. I'm starting to think it should have marshmallow cream inside, and I'll do buttercream for the frosting. You know, really show the customer how much sweetness we can pack into one cupcake."

Mrs. Cake grabbed a few boxes of cookies from the top shelf and chuckled. "I want you to know, Pinkie Pie, that no matter what happens with Sugarcube Corner, Mr. Cake and I are so glad you came to work here. Having you in the café has always been so much fun. You've come up with some of our best recipes, and you're always such a hard worker. You're like family."

"Wait, now you're talking as if we're definitely closing," Pinkie Pie said sadly. "I thought you were going to wait until the end of the month to see!"

"The end of the month is coming up soon...." Mrs. Cake shrugged. Then she stared off for a moment, a sad expression taking over her face.

Just then Rarity strode into the back room with a stack of extra napkins. Since business had slowed down, Mrs. Cake put her in charge of organizing the napkin holders. It took her three times longer than it would have taken anyone else as she straightened every corner and smoothed every fold to perfection, but she'd finally finished. She dropped the extras into a box beside the pantry.

"Maybe we could do something else, something bigger..." Pinkie tried.

"I don't know," Mrs. Cake said. "I loved karaoke night, but I don't think it's enough to save us in the long run. Besides, I don't know if my ears can handle that every week...."

"What about a big, super-fun party," Pinkie Pie said. "Isn't that worth a shot?"

"I love the idea of a fabulous party," Rarity chimed in.

Mrs. Cake perked up a little. Pinkie Pie knew the Cakes didn't want to close Sugarcube Corner. They all just had to keep trying until they found the thing that people were truly excited about. There had to be something they had that Butter's Bakery didn't.

"We could make it a huge, special party for Canterlot High students," Pinkie continued. "The Rainbooms can play, and we'll have CHS cupcakes and cookies, and it'll just be super-silly fun. We need them to see

that this is still *the* place to be after school. This will always be their real hangout."

But Rarity shook her head. "If you're going to have a party for Canterlot High students, it needs to be exclusive. Make it feel like the place to be, *if* the place to be is just out of reach. Guest lists. Invitation only. Velvet ropes and hashtags and a whole step-and-repeat area."

"Step and repeat?" Mrs. Cake asked. "I don't know what that is. . . ."

"Me neither," Pinkie Pie said, shrugging and scrunching her nose.

"Pinkie Pie! Come on!" Rarity laughed. "It's the photo backdrop area where you take pictures of people at events. They use these great, flattering flashes that make you look spectacular. Don't tell me you've never heard of it."

"Oh…" Pinkie Pie felt silly for not knowing. "It sounds familiar."

"Canterlot High students have come to expect greatness," Rarity continued. "Lavishness and Glamour with a capital *G*! Especially if you're trying to draw them away from Butter's with all its fancy cocoa and fireplaces."

Mrs. Cake took a deep breath. Pinkie knew she had been excited by the idea of a party, but then Rarity had to go and start talking about hashtags and step and whatevers. Now Mrs. Cake seemed totally overwhelmed. Why did everything have to be fancy and capital-*G* Glamorous? Couldn't they just throw a big party and have a ton of fun? Sugarcube Corner was a place for everyone.

"I'll think about it…" Mrs. Cake finally said before heading back into the café.

Pinkie Pie grabbed a spatula and started mixing some marshmallow cream with vanilla extract. She was so worried that Rarity would try to do this party the wrong way. She didn't understand the bakery, the Cakes, or the customers very well. Pinkie was sure that a super-fun party that was all about the good times—and not exclusivity—was the right way to go.

"One word," Rarity said as she flitted back out to the café. *"Exclusive."*

Pinkie gave the marshmallow cream another stir and frowned.

CHAPTER 10

Sugar on the Corner

Pinkie Pie set down the tray of hot chocolates in front of Fluttershy, Sunset Shimmer, Applejack, and Rainbow Dash. They'd been coming in every day after school, even when most Canterlot High students were at Butter's Bakery. Applejack had made it her personal mission to eat as many Sugarcube Corner cookies as she could.

"Where's Rarity?" Rainbow Dash asked as she dug into a piece of peach pie.

"I'm sure Rarity will be here any minute," Pinkie Pie said, trying not to sound too disappointed. Rarity was supposed to be there at three, but she was running late again.

Sunset Shimmer glanced over her shoulder at Mr. Cake, who was helping a customer pick out a sugar cookie for her young daughter. "Do you think there's still hope?" she asked, her voice uneven. "When will they officially decide?"

"I'm trying to get them to wait just one more week," Pinkie said. "I had this idea for a party, and I think if we could just—"

"I got it!" a familiar voice called out. They

turned to see Rarity striding toward them. *"Sugar...on the Corner..."*

"Um...what does that mean?" Pinkie Pie asked.

"Sugar on the Corner!" Rarity repeated. "It's a big idea; I think the biggest we've had. I think it can save Sugarcube Corner!"

"What can save Sugarcube Corner?" Mr. Cake came over to the table after he'd rung up the woman's cookie. He looked genuinely hopeful. His green eyes were bright.

"Everyone from Canterlot High used to come after school or on the weekends," Rarity explained. "Now they've started going to Butter's instead. But what if we did something so cool that they just decided they liked Sugarcube Corner more? What if it was *the* place to be?"

"How would we do that?" Mr. Cake seemed confused.

"Sugar on the Corner." Rarity swept her hands through the air in a dramatic gesture. "One night a week, Sugarcube Corner will admit only Canterlot High students. There will be tasty treats. There will be a dress code. There will be a band and a photo booth and no adults allowed. Well, except you and Mrs. Cake."

Pinkie Pie's eyes lit up! Rarity was following through with Pinkie's idea. But would Pinkie get any say...or any credit?

Mr. Cake paced back and forth. He put his hand on his chin. "I have to get the okay from Mrs. Cake, but I think it's worth a shot. We could do the first one this Friday. Is that enough time for you two to pull it together?"

"Of course." Pinkie Pie saw her chance to jump in. "I already have a ton of ideas."

"Well, great, then," Mr. Cake said. "We'll trust you two to plan the perfect night. I think…if this doesn't work, I don't know what will. I'm going to go find Mrs. Cake and tell her all about it."

As he left, Rarity turned to Pinkie Pie and grabbed both her hands. She shook them up and down with excitement. "I'm telling you—this is it!" she said. "We're going to plan the best party together!"

Pinkie tried hard to smile, but she wasn't convinced. Rarity wasn't always the best employee.…Would they really be able to pull it off?

CHAPTER 11

The Sugarcube Corner Planning Committee

Pinkie Pie looked at the to-do list she'd made the night before. As head of the Party Planning Committee at Canterlot High, she had organized dozens of unquestionably fun events: the Fall Formal, Blitzball Brunch (where prospective players could learn about the team), High Tea with Principal Celestia

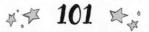

and Vice Principal Luna, and a fund-raiser for the Equestria Girls and Boys Club. If there was something Pinkie Pie did best, it was planning an amazing party.

She'd written a quick three-page list of the different desserts she wanted to have at Sugar on the Corner. The Rainbooms would play—that was obvious—and she made notes about getting cute paper napkins and cups so they wouldn't have to worry about kids breaking the nice ceramic ones. She envisioned everything covered in her favorite color: pink! *Pretty pink stationery invites with fluffy cupcakes on them,* she wrote at the bottom of the list. *A banner that says* SUGAR ON THE CORNER?

"You're not going to believe who I hired to play on Friday night," Rarity said as she sat down. They were at one of the sidewalk tables outside Sugarcube Corner. Mr. and Mrs. Cake had given them the afternoon off so they could finalize the event. That, and the café had been so slow that the Cakes barely needed any help.

"Oh, I thought the Rainbooms were going to play…" Pinkie Pie said, trying to smile through her disappointment. She was sure that Rarity had a good idea if she'd already hired the band, but…was this the first sign that she and Rarity really weren't on the same page?

"Well, I love the Rainbooms—you know that—but we've played at Sugarcube Corner a half-dozen times. We need to start thinking bigger…an act that will draw a crowd. Something new and hip and edgy. Like…the Comeback Kids!"

"The Comeback Kids?" Uh-oh. This

party was supposed to be lighthearted, and fluffy, and *fun*. And the Comeback Kids almost exclusively played sad ballads about broken hearts. "I just don't think they're—"

"I already booked them." Rarity shrugged. "They needed to know right then because it's such short notice...."

Pinkie let out a sigh. Maybe the Rainbooms wouldn't play, but that didn't mean they couldn't use the rest of her ideas. She'd just have to reimagine some of the details to fit the new band.

"So I was thinking desserts everywhere," Pinkie Pie said. "We could make a three-tiered cake with the Canterlot High colors and the mascot. Or—*ohhh!* Maybe just a giant Wondercolt! Miniature cupcakes and cookies and hot chocolate for everyone. Basically, sugar *everywhere*! I really want to show off how good the desserts are at Sugar-cube Corner."

"I know," Rarity said slowly. "But I was thinking of this more as…just a really cool party. We can have all the refreshments at one table and kids will get a cupcake or cake when they want some, but we should think of different things to raise our profile. Bigger ideas. A photo booth, the step and repeat. I want everyone using the hashtag #SugarontheCorner."

"But Sugarcube Corner is a dessert place," Pinkie tried. "Shouldn't that be what we focus on? I was thinking we could give each kid a goody bag with miniature cook-ies. The bag could be sparkly!"

"A goody bag?" Rarity's eyes went wide. "That feels so third grade! Pinkie Pie, you have to think *cool*. Exclusive."

"Okay, see, you keep saying that word, *exclusive*." Pinkie Pie started to delicately make her point. "But what do you really mean by that?"

"People should feel lucky they're invited, and lucky if they get in," Rarity went on. "Sugarcube Corner can hold only fifty people, tops. Not everyone is going to be able to come."

"But that's the whole point of Sugarcube Corner! Everyone is welcome."

Pinkie could hear her voice rising. Why were they having a party that didn't match up with what Sugarcube Corner was? Why did Rarity want to turn it into something else? One of the best things about the café was how warm and welcoming it was.

"Well, not on Friday nights. I'm going to

tell Sunset Shimmer and Twilight Sparkle to do the inviting. Nothing official. I want them to just 'spread the word' about the party, and be very selective about who they tell," Rarity said. "Oh, #showyoursugar! That's a great one for the photo booth! People can post that on their networks!"

Pinkie Pie stared down at her to-do list. "So basically I should just make some desserts...?"

"Yes! Perfect, darling! But not Canterlot High–themed ones," Rarity said. Just then her cell phone rang, and she grabbed it from her purse. She stood and turned her back to Pinkie Pie as she picked it up. "It's the person from the photo booth place. I have to get this. Just—make those desserts! Plan for about fifty kids!"

She strode off down the sidewalk, saying something about "flattering lighting." Pinkie Pie's stomach was twisted into knots. She was the one who was head of the CHS Party Planning Committee, but Rarity wasn't listening to a word she said. What about the cupcake hats Pinkie Pie wanted to make? Or the silent auction she wanted to have for a Sugarcube Corner–themed birthday party? And she didn't care what Rarity said—it was a proven fact that everyone loved goody bags.

"I will make those desserts," Pinkie Pie said as she underlined that item on her to-do list. But then she continued down it, underlining the other items, too. "And make the cupcake hats...and the goody bags...and get those paper plates and cups...."

She'd worked at Sugarcube Corner for

years, and she knew the place better than Rarity did. Pinkie understood what kind of party Rarity wanted, she did. But that didn't mean she agreed with it.

They'd just have to find a way to do everything both of them wanted to do, all at one super-fun party.

CHAPTER
12

Two Parties in One

"All right, Sugarcube Corner is officially closed for the night." Mr. Cake taped a sign to the door that said CLOSED FOR A PRIVATE EVENT. "Mrs. Cake and I will finish frosting those cupcakes, Pinkie Pie. You guys just holler if you need anything."

"Great, we will!" Pinkie said, striding over to Rarity. She set a few big boxes on the table in the center of the room and began unloading her supplies. "I made some cupcake hats and this great banner. Look at all the little details!"

She rolled the banner out on the table. It said SUGAR ON THE CORNER in big, loopy script. Then she'd hand-painted different desserts around it: chocolate chip cookies and pink-frosted cupcakes and slices of key lime pie. The cupcake hats she'd made out of papier-mâché. She'd put elastic string on them so it looked as if you were wearing a cupcake on your head!

Rarity went pale. "*Ummmm...*I thought you were just making the desserts?"

"Well, yeah. We needed some decorations, too!"

"But I have decorations." Rarity looked confused.

There was a knock on the door. Pinkie Pie ran to open it, and in walked all eight of the Comeback Kids. They'd come early to practice their set for the night. Two workers were right behind them, carrying the materials for the photo booth. Rarity immediately went into planning mode.

"You can set up your musical equipment in that corner," she said, pointing to one side of the café. "And we'll put the photo booth right here by the counter."

"But where are we going to put the banner? And the cupcake table?" Pinkie Pie asked. "I had this whole setup for the hats, too. We can place them on a long table against the wall so people can pick out their own."

The Comeback Kids and the workers were standing there, watching them argue. They were holding their heavy equipment. "We don't got all day," one of the workers grumbled.

"Hey! Here's an idea…" Pinkie said, sensing the tension. "Why don't we just have two themes? One party; *both* visions!"

"Um, I suppose that could work," Rarity said. "Okay, boys. You can just put everything on this side of the room."

"Great!" Pinkie Pie agreed. "I can decorate everything on this side."

Pinkie Pie started setting up around the counter and front tables while the band and photo booth workers set up in the back part of the café. She was sure this plan would work. Pinkie hung the banner above the counter, right where she had imagined it would be, and lined up the cupcake hats on a table against the wall. She was bringing out the huge, three-tiered Wondercolt cake when the rest of their friends walked in.

"Wow," Rainbow Dash said, glancing from one side of the room to the other. "This is like two parties in one."

"Cool photo booth!" Sunset Shimmer said, running inside. She and Fluttershy took three silly pictures in a row, and the machine shot out a photo strip. The background had #showyoursugar written all over it.

Rarity's side of the room had silver- and gold-star confetti scattered on the floor, and she'd put a velvet rope outside the door and had the step and repeat there. The Comeback Kids played a few notes, warming up their instruments.

"Come see the Wondercolt cake!" Pinkie

Pie said, pulling Rainbow Dash and Apple-jack over to it. "I made it in three days. Doesn't it look just like the statue in front of Canterlot High?"

"It definitely does," Applejack said. But she kept glancing over her shoulder to see what was happening on the other side of the room. Twilight Sparkle was talking to some of the Comeback Kids. The lead singer, Red Forest, was a cute junior from the next town over. There was a rumor he used to model for the *Canterlot Gazette* ads.

Pinkie Pie grabbed Rainbow Dash's hand and led her to the cupcake hats. "Try one on!" she said. "They're so fun, aren't they?"

Rainbow Dash put a chocolate cupcake on her head, looping the band under her chin. Pinkie thought she looked adorable.

For some weird reason, Rainbow Dash took it off just a few seconds later.

"You have to walk the step and repeat, friends!" Rarity called out. She made Twilight and Fluttershy follow her out to the front of the café. She already had a photographer taking pictures of the Sugar on the Corner backdrop.

Feeling a little sad, Pinkie Pie watched her friends go. She was glad Rarity's stuff was popular...but why did they like Rarity's decorations better than hers? Twilight was practically swooning over Red Forest. Pinkie glanced at her Wondercolt cake, which had taken hours to design. This was the first party Pinkie had thrown that just wasn't any fun at all.

"How come the café is decorated so differently?" Sunset Shimmer asked, glancing from one side of the room to the other. She walked down the line in the middle where Rarity's confetti stopped. "It's kind of… *weird*."

"Yes, it is…." Mrs. Cake came out of the back room holding the stack of paper plates and napkins Pinkie Pie had bought. They were covered with tiny chocolate chip cookies. She took in the café. "It feels like two different parties with two different themes."

Seeing Mrs. Cake through the window, Rarity darted back inside. "Well, we ended up having different visions, so we thought we would do both. That's my side of the room, with the photo booth. I wanted glitz and glamour. And Pinkie Pie wanted more of a sugar-and-sweets theme. Both are fabulous, obviously."

"That's very true, but maybe we can

make it feel like one party instead of two?" Mrs. Cake suggested.

"Which party do you want it to be, though? Should we stick with the dessert theme?" Pinkie Pie felt a little nervous asking the question. She wanted Mrs. Cake to like what she'd done, of course. She wanted the whole café to be decorated the way she'd envisioned. Rarity's party was "cool," but it wasn't sweet and warm and sugary like Sugarcube Corner.

"Let's just go with the glitz and glamour theme," Mrs. Cake finally said. "We already have the photo booth and velvet rope and everything. Maybe we could do a sweets-themed party another night. It's a great idea, Pinkie; it really is."

Mrs. Cake offered her a small, sad smile, then returned to the back room. Pinkie Pie felt everyone watching her, even the Come-back Kids. She swore she heard Red Forest whisper something about her cupcake hats.

She'd never been more embarrassed in her whole life.

CHAPTER
13

Inspiration and Perspiration

"You guys can help Rarity decorate the rest of the café," Pinkie Pie said, her cheeks red. She couldn't take it anymore; all the sadness and disappointment from the past few weeks had built up and she felt as if she were going to burst. "I'm going to go finish frosting the cupcakes and make sure we have enough cookies ready, and bake some more…because this is a bakery and that's what I do. I don't need to plan some raging, super-cool party."

She turned on her heel and went into the back room. Her heart was pounding. For a moment she thought she might cry, but then she saw Mr. and Mrs. Cake in the back office and she tried her best not to. She couldn't tell them how devastated she was by the thought of losing Sugarcube Corner. She couldn't tell them how much she wanted to be a big part of saving her second home…or how much it upset her that her ideas only seemed to make things worse.

Pinkie Pie picked up the bowl of marshmallow cream from the fridge. She dumped in a few teaspoons of vanilla extract and mixed it up. Then she slid a tray of whole marshmallows into the oven, right under the broiler. She wanted them to get nice and toasted brown. She riffled through the cabinets, looking for other ingredients she could use. She pulled out a pack of sliced almonds, crushed them up, and then mixed them in, too.

Baking always calmed her down. For so long, Sugarcube Corner had been her escape whenever she needed it. If she didn't do well on a test or had a fight with a friend or had a hard day at school or felt sad for any other reason, she could always come to Sugarcube Corner to relax. If she was being totally honest, working with Rarity had made that harder. Maybe it was because of the new pressure with Butter's Bakery, or maybe it was because she and Rarity didn't work the same way. But she felt as if Sugarcube Corner were slipping away from her. In some ways, it was already gone.

The timer on the oven went off, and she pulled out the tray of toasted marshmallows. They were a perfect golden brown, and they smelled delicious. She picked up a few with a fork and tossed them into the bowl of marshmallow cream, stirring them around and around. If she put the mixture in a piping bag, she could squeeze it right into the center of the cupcake. She'd use it for the top, too. She didn't have time to make a fresh batch of buttercream frosting.

"Baking away…" Mrs. Cake said as she

stepped out of the office. Mr. Cake was right behind her. "There's still a few dozen cupcakes for the party, if you want to frost those, too. I think we have enough cookies already."

"I'll definitely frost them," Pinkie said. She didn't look up from the bowl.

"Pinkie, I'm sorry if before—" started Mrs. Cake.

"It's okay," Pinkie said, and she meant it. "I think these last few weeks have just been difficult for me. I want to stay positive, but it's hard."

"For us, too," Mr. Cake said. "It's very scary."

"I just…" Pinkie could feel the tears in her eyes. "I really love this place."

"We do, too. So much," Mrs. Cake said,

wrapping her arm around Pinkie's shoulders. "Why don't we frost some of these cupcakes together? For old time's sake."

"I'd like that," Pinkie said.

Mr. Cake pulled a few trays from the fridge. They worked quietly, sometimes laughing at different memories from Sugarcube Corner. There was the time Pinkie had accidentally made a "cat" cake when she misheard a woman who'd said "car." Or the times Mr. Cake put on music, and they danced while they cleaned up the café. Mrs. Cake had once slipped and tossed a bowl of batter in the air, and it had gone all over Pinkie's head. She had picked bits of chocolate out of her ears for days.

Pinkie piped the marshmallow filling into each of her mocha cupcakes, letting it calm her down. She hoped everything would go perfectly tonight, even if she hadn't planned the party. And, most important, she hoped there'd be more days like this to come, with her in Sugarcube Corner, enjoying its sweetness.

CHAPTER 14

Making Up Is Hard to Do

A half hour had passed before Rarity finally came into the back room. The Cakes had returned to their office to go through the paperwork for the week. Pinkie Pie was arranging the last of the peanut butter cookies on a plate.

"Can we talk?" Rarity asked. She seemed nervous.

Outside, the Comeback Kids were finishing their warm-up. Pinkie Pie had actually enjoyed the last few songs she'd heard. She kept bopping her head to the music. "Sure," she said softly.

"I feel as if you're mad at me for taking over the party planning," Rarity started. She set aside the plate of cookies and began arranging the mocha cupcakes on another platter. "I just had this vision of how it would go. I want this night to be the best it can be."

"So do I," Pinkie Pie said. "But I had a vision, too. And I felt as if you just thought all my ideas were silly."

"Oh, that's not true at all," Rarity tried. She leaned both elbows on the table and watched Pinkie Pie closely.

"Remember outside? When we were talking?" Pinkie asked. "You kept shouting out hashtags, even though I'd already told you the theme I wanted. And you booked the band without even asking me first."

Rarity tilted her head to one side. She seemed to be considering it. "I guess you're right," she admitted. "But I really know what this night should be. I know you've been a party planner for ages, and you've worked at Sugarcube Corner much longer than I have, but you have to trust me on this."

"I do trust you, deep, deep, *deep* down. But…it's just kind of hard because I'm worried the Cakes will lose everything. And"— as soon as Pinkie Pie thought it, she knew it was true—"that I'll lose everything. I don't know what I'll do if Sugarcube Corner closes. I love this place so much."

"Which is why it's almost better that I plan the party," Rarity said. "I can really see all the potential here. Look, I know I'm not that great at keeping track of pickup orders or getting here on time, or…um…*working*, really. But I think I did a really great job for tonight. I think we're going to be okay."

"Really?" Pinkie Pie felt better just hearing those words.

"Really."

"I guess it was hard for me, too…." Pinkie Pie tried to find the right way to say it. "Because Mr. and Mrs. Cake really like you. And I'm used to being the person they rely on for everything."

"I know," Rarity said. "Can I show you something?"

She grabbed Pinkie Pie's hand and pulled her to the doorway. Pinkie Pie stared out at the café. It was hardly recognizable. It was shimmering with silver and gold stars. Twilight Sparkle was adding gold streamers to the step and repeat outside, and the Comeback Kids had brought in their own lighting system. There were tiny gold lights twinkling throughout the room. The ceiling looked like the night sky.

"Wow. It really does look great." Pinkie meant it.

She turned to her friend and wrapped her arms around her. It felt good to agree with her friend again. With all the little things piling up between them, it had been easy to forget they were on the same side.

"Thanks for all the help," Pinkie said. "I

think a capital-*G* Glamorous party might be just what Sugarcube Corner needs."

"Fingers crossed," Rarity said.

"Fingers and toes and eyes crossed," Pinkie agreed, making a silly face.

Rarity laughed, and that's when Pinkie Pie was sure they'd really made up.

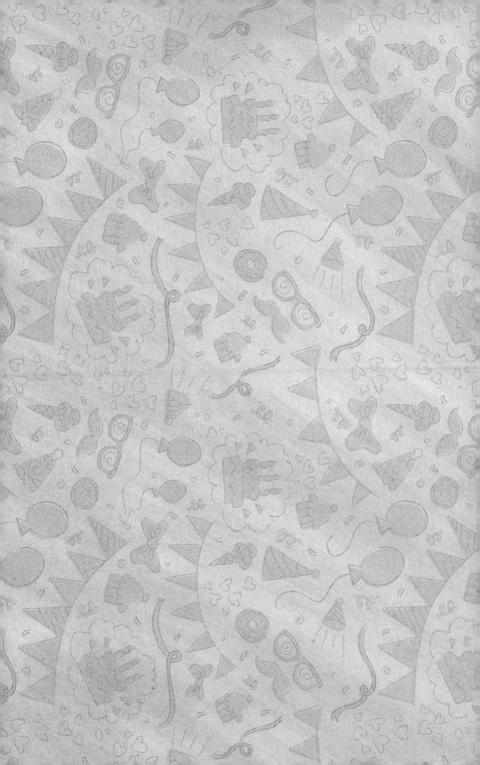

CHAPTER 15

Taste Testing

"What are those?" Rarity asked, stepping back into the kitchen. She went over to the tray of mocha cupcakes Pinkie Pie had frosted. She'd been so happy chatting with Mr. and Mrs. Cake that she'd made three dozen of them without even blinking.

"That's the recipe…" Pinkie Pie said. "Or what I have so far. The mocha cocoa cupcake. I'd hoped it would be ready to sell at Sugar on the Corner, but I don't know. Feels as if we're running out of time."

Rarity closed her eyes and breathed in. "These smell so good. Like campfires and s'mores and hot cocoa. All the best things. Can I try one?"

"Of course." Pinkie Pie leaned on the counter. "But just be warned. It isn't the finished recipe. There's still work to do. I think maybe I have to tweak the frosting a bit or even—"

"*Mmmmmm….*" Rarity raised her eyebrows as she savored the first bite. She took another bite, then another. She almost ate the whole thing before she spoke. "You don't have to do anything else. This is the best cupcake I've ever tasted."

"Really?" Pinkie knew Rarity wanted to make her feel better, but she really didn't have to go this far. *The best cupcake she'd ever tasted?*

"Really. We should do a taste test. I'm telling you, it's true." Rarity popped the last bite into her mouth. Then she cupped her hand over her mouth and called out into the café. "Rainbow Dash, Twilight! You have to try this cupcake for us!"

The two girls darted into the kitchen. Twilight had been so busy decorating for the party that she still had some streamers in her arms. Rarity picked up two more mocha cupcakes and passed them to Rainbow Dash and Twilight. They each ate them in just a few bites.

"Whoa, that is incredible," Rainbow Dash said. She reached for another one, but Pinkie grabbed her hand. She'd only made so many!

"Seriously—so good," Twilight agreed. "Who made that? Mrs. Cake?"

"Pinkie Pie did! She's a true culinary genius!" Rarity clapped and cheered. "I want to shout it from the rooftops! This is the best thing I've ever eaten."

Pinkie Pie's cheeks turned red. She knew the cupcake was good, but she didn't realize how good until that very moment. She saw it sometimes at the bakery. When a batch of a certain cookie came out just right, people would go crazy for it. She'd actually seen a lady jump up and down over a particularly delicious piece of pumpkin pie.

"Wait..." Pinkie Pie went into the fridge

and looked at the trays they hadn't yet iced. She still had one more, and then the three dozen cupcakes she'd already frosted, minus the few her friends had just eaten. "This is incredible. I have an idea...."

CHAPTER 16

The Mocha Marvel

"I had perfect timing on this, and I didn't even mean to!" Pinkie Pie said, glancing around at her friends. "Do we still have those cookie boxes, Rarity? The ones you ordered that…"

Pinkie Pie was trying to be nice, so she

didn't finish her thought. The first week Rarity had worked at Sugarcube Corner, she made a big purchase of cookie boxes, only she ordered the wrong size. When they'd come in, they were way too small— three inches tall and three inches wide. Pinkie Pie had told her she could give them away, but Rarity had been stubborn. She kept telling Pinkie she'd find something to use them for.

"I put them right here." Rarity grabbed a stack of flat boxes from a bottom cabinet. She set them down on the counter.

Pinkie folded the top one into shape. Then she put one of the mocha cupcakes inside and closed it. It was a perfect fit.

"I see where you're going with this…" Rarity said, excited. She ran into the other room and came back with some silver stars and ribbons. She scribbled the words *The Mocha Marvel* on a star, then wrapped the box with ribbon and tucked the star in the top. It looked very professional.

"Hmm...the Mocha Marvel." Pinkie Pie repeated the name. It did have a good ring to it. "We can give these out at the party tonight."

"Or even better—we'll sell them," Rarity said. "And we don't have enough for everyone."

"Exclusive." Pinkie Pie laughed, echoing Rarity's favorite word.

"Exclusive!" Rarity agreed. "This is the new big thing in Equestria, and no one but us knows it yet. Forget cake pops or cronuts—the Mocha Marvel is where it's at."

"A phenomenon!" Pinkie Pie smiled.

"Let's get these wrapped up. We don't

have much time," Rarity said as Sunset Shimmer and Fluttershy rushed in to help. They folded the boxes as fast as they could.

The friends started their own little production line. Once Twilight Sparkle and Rainbow Dash had finished making a box, they passed it to Rarity, who put a cupcake in as gently as she could. Pinkie Pie frosted the rest of the cupcakes while Fluttershy and Sunset Shimmer attached the ribbons and labels. Applejack mostly just stood there and acted as an unofficial taste tester. She swiped a spoonful of frosting whenever she could.

They kept at it for a while, filling box after box. When they were finally done, they had almost fifty boxes, each with one cupcake inside. Just enough so kids would have to really scramble if they wanted to try a Mocha Marvel for themselves.

It was hard for Pinkie Pie to admit, but Rarity had been right about the whole "exclusive" thing. It was better to have more demand than supply.

They went to the Sugarcube Corner bathroom to get changed and do their hair, and Rarity was more excited than she had been the whole week. She kept coming up with a million different hashtags.

"#MarvelousNight, #MarvelingTonight, #IMarvel, #MochaMarvelMe..." she said as she brushed her hair. She stuck a bow in the side and raised her eyebrows, as if she were having a *Eureka!* moment. "#MochaMarvelMe! That's the one!"

"I love it," Fluttershy said.

"So shareable!" Twilight Sparkle agreed.

Pinkie Pie tugged on one of her favorite dresses, which had a big pink skirt and brighter pink flouncy blouse. She wore her hair down, and Sunset Shimmer helped her with the back of it, making sure all her curls fell right.

When she was all done getting ready, Pinkie stared at her reflection in the small mirror, happier than she had felt in a long time. The party would start in just a half hour. Kids would be lined up outside the door of Sugarcube Corner, excited about the café and its food and all the fun they'd have there. They'd take pictures in the photo booth and make social media posts about how cool Sugar on the Corner was. Then they'd eat her special cupcake, the recipe she'd worked on for months, and they'd love it.

She smiled at herself, her blue eyes bright with possibility.

She had a feeling it was going to be a truly *marvelous* night.

CHAPTER 17

A Showstopper

The Comeback Kids danced around as they played their first song, "You're the One." Red Forest shimmied and shook when he belted out the lyrics. *"You know you're smart and you're in my heart; and you're the one,"* he sang. *"You're in my heart; you are the* onnnnne."

A dozen Canterlot High girls were in the

front row cheering him on. It was a little sappy for Pinkie Pie's taste, but she understood why everyone loved them so much. They were all really cute, and their music was genuinely catchy. Since the party had started, she hadn't stopped nodding her head. Every song made her want to get up and dance.

"You were right," she said, pulling Rarity over to her. "If we were playing with the Sonic Rainbooms, we would be performing all night. We wouldn't have the chance to enjoy this."

"I know, and it's been so great, right?" Rarity asked.

"Better than I ever could've imagined." Pinkie glanced through the window at the line to get in. Mr. Cake was standing at the door. He was flustered by the line of dressed-up Canterlot High kids asking him over and over again when they could go inside. He could let only one kid in after a kid left. They were already at capacity!

Dozens of people had taken photos in the photo booth, and even more had gone through the step and repeat. All night, Pinkie had seen pictures popping up everywhere on social media. Everyone was talking about how great Sugarcube Corner was. People were even speculating about what the "big surprise" would be.

The song ended, and Red Forest wiped his sweaty bangs out of his eyes. "I want to thank you all for coming out," he said breathlessly. "You've all been wondering what we're here for tonight, and it's a little thing called the Mocha Marvel."

The room broke out into whispers. Red

Forest seemed to be enjoying the drama because he let people go on for a little bit, trying to figure out what he meant.

"Look, I've tried this thing," Red Forest finally said. "And it is the best cupcake I've ever had. I mean, it's not really a cupcake... it's a piece of heaven. And it's available now at Sugarcube Corner. There's only a limited supply tonight, though, so line up at the counter if you're interested."

The whole party shifted. Everyone darted over to the counter, where Sunset Shimmer and Mrs. Cake had all the boxes piled high. Mrs. Cake rang up the orders as fast as she could, but as soon as they'd given a box to one person, there was someone right behind them asking for another.

Kids began ripping open the boxes with an intensity Pinkie Pie had never seen before. Ribbons and stars were all over the floor. "Whoa! I can't believe how good it is!" one girl with a high bun yelled. "You have to try it."

The girl's friend waited in line, looking nervous that she might not get one. As more people left the photo booth or step and repeat to get their Mocha Marvel, the Comeback Kids started the next song. It was a fast number called "You've Got What It Takes."

As Red Forest belted out the first line, Pinkie Pie swore he looked over at her and winked.

CHAPTER
18

Lines Out the Door

Pinkie Pie had set up an assembly line in the back room. Even with Pinkie, Rarity, Fluttershy, Rainbow Dash, and Applejack working together, they still couldn't put the boxes together fast enough. It had been almost a week since Sugar on the Corner, and the demand for the Mocha Marvel had not slowed down at all.

"My hands hurt," Fluttershy said as she folded her hundredth box of the day.

"Mine too," Applejack added. She was in charge of wrapping the ribbon around the boxes and tying it in a bow.

"That was the last one!" Pinkie Pie said. She'd just piped the filling into the final Mocha Marvel. She'd been baking a hundred a day, and even that wasn't enough to keep up with all the people who'd come into the café.

After the party, word had spread quickly. At first it was mainly Canterlot High kids who'd come in, asking for their newest dessert. But then it seemed as if everyone in town had heard about it. There were young moms and their kids, a senior group from Canterlot Gardens, and Mrs. Cake's knitting club. Just this afternoon a whole pack of Crystal Prep students had walked into Sugarcube Corner, asking what a Mocha Marvel was. Pinkie Pie had been so surprised she'd dropped a mug of hot chocolate.

The best part was, people hadn't just tried it once. They were coming back for more. There was one freshman from Canterlot who'd come in every day that week to eat a Mocha Marvel after school. Then there was Feathers Grey, who seemed the most addicted of anyone. He'd started eating two cupcakes whenever he read his book, and he always took two cupcakes home with him to share with his whole family.

"How are we doing back here?" called

out Mr. Cake. He came in and picked up another big stack of boxes to take out to the front. "Thanks for pitching in, girls. The way this is going, we should be able to give you shifts this whole month."

"I don't know if my hands can take it anymore," Fluttershy said softly.

Mrs. Cake peeked in her head. She looked happier than Pinkie had ever seen her, her smile big and bright. "Don't work too hard, girls!" she called out. "The next Sugar on the Corner is just two days away. You have to save some of your energy for dancing!"

Pinkie Pie and Rarity each grabbed an armful of boxes and brought them out front. They stacked them on a new table they'd set up just to hold the supply of Mocha Marvels. Every seat in the place was taken. It was mostly Canterlot High students, but there were new faces, too. It seemed as if customers became regulars pretty quickly after trying the cupcake.

"It worked," Rarity said, staring out at the crowd. "I mean, I thought it would, but it really did!"

"You were right." Pinkie Pie smiled as she looked at the line out the door. It had been like this every afternoon since Sugar on the Corner.

"We both were right," Rarity corrected. "If you hadn't kept baking, doing what you do best, none of this would've happened. You saved Sugarcube Corner, Pinkie Pie."

Pinkie Pie waved her off, trying to dismiss it, but she couldn't stop beaming with pride. In fact, she hadn't stopped smiling the whole week. As she darted around the café, clearing tables and chatting with customers, she felt lighter than ever.

Sugarcube Corner was here to stay. And nothing, not even a Butter's Bakery with fireplaces, could change that.

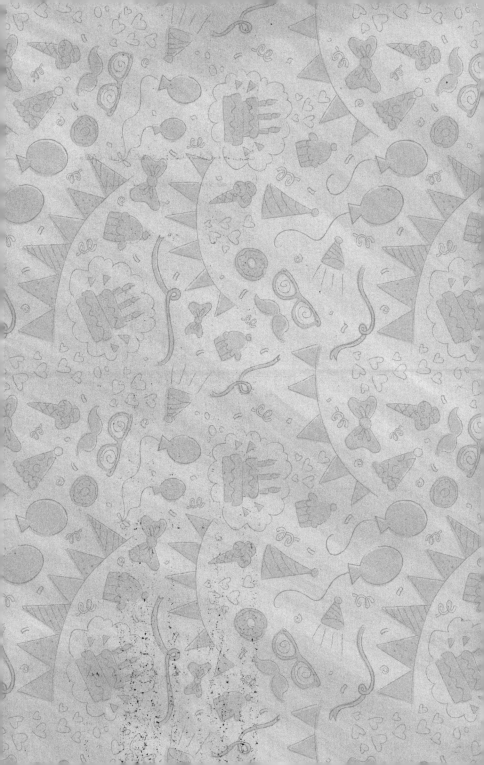

Pinkie Pie's Signature Style

Pinkie Pie is a girly-girl through and through. Not only is Pinkie a party planner extraordinaire and lover of glitter, she is a *feminine fashion maven*! Her wardrobe is all pinks, ruffles, bows, tulles, and lace.

Pinkie loves a skirt and has never met a heel she was afraid of. Her closet is as *light and bright* as her personality, and she always has a handbag to match.

Not only does Pinkie Pie have a feminine aesthetic, she is also *adventurous and bold* with the details. She loves to *mix patterns* as long as they have some of her favorite color: *pink*!

She also uses different fabrics and finishes to pull together her outfits. Pinkie always keeps it interesting!

There are so many things to love about Pinkie Pie's style, but what makes her so fashionable is that *she never takes herself too seriously*. Fun always seems to be at the top of her priority list. Yes, she is always put together and accessorized to perfection, but she also clearly loves to keep things totally *playful*.

Are You a Pinkie Pie?

Let's talk about how you can re-create Pinkie's look with some key pieces.

Signature Color

Shutterstock.com/Africa Studio

Shutterstock.com/Tarzhanova

The number one rule of Pinkie Pie's wardrobe is pink, pink, **PINK**! She wears it; she layers it; she accessorizes with it.…She rocks it! Without a doubt, pink is her signature color. Pinkie loves how many shades are available. She can go with a pastel or a neon—and every hue in between! Having a signature color makes completing a look so much easier because all the tones tend to look great together. Bold skirt with a pastel top? Yes! Pale-pink dress with neon shoes? All day. Pinkie loves every shade of pink and knows exactly how to wear them together.

Feminine Details

Some girls love leather and studs. Some love denim and boots. Pinkie Pie loves *tulle and lace. Ruffles, beading,* and *bling* are all ultra-feminine touches that make this girly-girl really feel in her element. When choosing her wardrobe, Pinkie always thinks about the overall picture. Do all her pieces go with pink? Obviously. But they also all give off

Shutterstock.com/Maffi

the same *feminine vibe*. Her skirts are never tight or fitted—instead, she chooses bottoms with **volume and flare**. Even the tiniest detail can make any addition perfect for Pinkie Pie. A subtle bow or tiny jewel can take something basic and make it a feminine piece.

So Many Accessories

What does a girl who loves accessories need? Options—and tons of them! Pinkie Pie has a closet full of **shoes**, **scarves**, **bags**, and **coats**, and drawers full of **jewelry** and **headbands**. Even with all these options, there is one common theme in her accessory game: **variety**. She is constantly finding new ways to showcase her sense of style. Instead of a simple pink purse, she uses a *sequined bag* or throws on a *pink floral jacket and polka-dotted shoes*. Pinkie Pie's outfits are never complete without the perfect statement-making accessories.

FUN

And finally, all Pinkie Pie fans know that she lives for **FUN**! Pinkie knows how to bring *excitement and smiles* into every part of her life—especially style.

Shutterstock.com/Karkas

It might be a rad shoe in an *unexpected pop of color*. Or it could be a *bouncy skirt with layers to spare*. Whatever Pinkie Pie chooses to wear, she will make you feel joy in every outfit she puts on.

Can you spot the pieces of girly-girl clothing in Pinkie Pie's wardrobe?

Now it's your turn to style Pinkie Pie! Draw her a new outfit!

Time to accessorize!
Add some Pinkie Pie flair to these simple pieces.

It's time for some fun at the mall!
Fill out your Pinkie Pie-
inspired shopping list.

-
-
-
-
-
-
-
-

What would be Pinkie Pie's biggest fashion Dos and Don'ts?

DOs

_____

_____

_____

DON'Ts

_____

_____

_____

Create three outfits for Pinkie Pie using the pieces below!

Do you have a signature color like Pinkie Pie? Why is it your favorite?

About the Stylist

Laura Schuffman is a My Little Pony: Equestria Girls stylist. When she's not dressing Canterlot High's coolest friends, she also serves as a fashion stylist for a network television program. Her work has been featured in countless publications, magazine covers, advertising campaigns, and commercials around the world!

Did you like sharing sweets
with **Pinkie Pie**?

Then you'll **love** trying out for the
Blitzball team with **Rainbow Dash**!

Turn the page for a special look at

CHAPTER 1

Beehive Blitzers

"Run, faster, yes, *gooooo!*" Rainbow Dash cried. She stood up, her hands clutched in front of her as she watched the television screen. The Beehive Blitzers, her favorite Blitzball team, were playing in the world championship against BlitzBoom. There were only thirty seconds left in the game.

Lightning Swift, one of the Beehive's fastest players, was dribbling toward the goal.

Applejack peeked out through her fingers. "I don't think I can watch...."

The score was tied, eighteen to eighteen. This one goal would mean winning or going into overtime. Rainbow Dash couldn't bear the thought of a shoot-out. It felt like such a random way to end the season. All that work, for what?

"Yes, you're so close," Rainbow Dash said as Lightning raised his hand, about to shoot the ball into the net. She reached into her pocket and felt for her lucky Beehive key chain. As soon as she'd bought it, the Beehive Blitzers had started winning, and their winning streak hadn't ended since. Just holding it made her feel better.

Everyone in Rainbow Dash's living room held her breath. Lightning took the shot, and one of the BlitzBoomers dove toward it. He reached out his hand, but the ball slipped past his fingers. Everyone cheered as it hit the back of the net.

"Twenty to eighteen!" Applejack threw her arms around Rainbow Dash. "We won!"

Comet Chaser, the Beehive's coach, ran onto the field, and his team enveloped him in a hug. Rainbow Dash and Applejack bounced up and down on their heels. Even Twilight Sparkle did a little dance, excited about the win. Rainbow Dash had known the key chain was a good-luck charm— she'd keep it in a safe place until the following season, when she'd make sure the Beehive Blitzers won again.

Rarity was smiling, but she didn't seem as impressed. She'd spent half the game talking to Fluttershy and Sunset Shimmer about a new dress she was sewing. She was having trouble figuring out what kind of pleats to use on the skirt. Rainbow Dash knew that not all her friends loved Blitzball, and none of them could love it as much as she did, but she'd planned a party for the championship game anyway. She'd served cupcakes with black and gold frosting (the Beehive's colors) and hung a banner over the television. She'd worn her Beehive jersey, the one with Lightning's name and number, and she'd had everyone else wear the team's colors. Rarity would get into the Beehive Blitzers spirit eventually—Rainbow Dash *just knew* she would. Wasn't her excitement contagious?

"The only sad thing is I have to wait a whole eight months before the season starts again," Rainbow Dash said. "What am I going to do with my weekends until then?"

"You can hang out with us," Twilight Sparkle said. "We'll be happy to have you back."

"Was it really that bad?" Rainbow Dash asked.

Fluttershy nodded. "We've barely seen you in the last two months!"

Rainbow Dash blushed. It was true, she had gotten a little obsessed with Blitzball this season. She loved how fast the game moved. The ball was dribbled and passed up the field and shot in the net, then it flew back to the other side of the field. Players stole the ball in really inventive, graceful ways. And the game was totally unpredictable.

Everything could change in an instant, which was so fun to watch.

Lately most of her weekends had been dedicated to watching the league games. Sure, the Beehive Blitzers were her favorite team, but she also loved watching the Larkspurs, the Tiny Titans, and the BlitzBolts. Well, if she were really being honest, she liked watching any team except the Rain Kings. They were the Beehive's biggest rival.

"Great game," Applejack said, grabbing her jean jacket. "Are you wearin' your jersey to school on Monday?"

"You bet," Rainbow Dash said.

"I should get a jersey, too," Sunset Shimmer chimed in. "After that game, I'm officially a Beehive fan. Lightning was all—" She took a few quick steps to the right, then pretended to spike the ball into the net. "It was incredible!"

"A snack for the road..." Pinkie Pie said, taking a cupcake on her way out. "We'll see you Monday, Rainbow Dash!"

When all her friends were gone, Rainbow Dash climbed the stairs to her bedroom. She looked at the three posters on her wall. One was of Lightning Swift, the best player on the Beehive Blitzers. One was of the whole team, and the third was of Oak Arrow, one of her other favorite players.

"Awesome work, guys," she said to them, smiling up at the posters. Then she grabbed the round purple pillow from off her bed. She darted around her room, pretending she was Lightning. She couldn't help wondering what it would be like to be that good at Blitzball. To weave in and out of the other players, dribbling and ducking, passing and shooting. She ran toward her desk, pretending it was the goal.

"She shoots, she scores!" she yelled, tossing the pillow under the desk. She did a small victory lap with her hands raised high in the air. Then she picked up the pillow, ready to do it all over again.

CHAPTER 2

Go Time

Monday came, and it felt as if Rainbow Dash talked to everyone about the championship game. A boy who sat next to her in chemistry, Forest Thunder, was also a Beehive Blitzer fan. They spent the whole class passing notes back and forth about Lightning, debating over which plays were his best.

Now she was in her last class, the minutes ticking by until the end of the day. Principal Celestia came on the loudspeaker to do the afternoon announcements.

"Congratulations to the girls' track team on their win against Crystal Prep Academy on Friday. Cloudy won the six-hundred-meter dash and…"

Rainbow Dash put her chin in her hands and stared out the window. She could barely pay attention to anything all day. Yesterday she'd started a Beehive Blitzers scrapbook, in which she'd placed news articles and pictures from the whole season. It had taken her forever just to do a few pages, but she couldn't wait to get back to work this afternoon. She'd found this really cool gold foil at the craft store to use behind the photos.

"Rainbow Dash!" Twilight Sparkle said,

nudging Rainbow Dash in the side. "Did you hear that?"

She pointed to the loudspeaker at the front of the room. Principal Celestia went on. "We're obviously thrilled to be part of this amazing opportunity. Now that their season is over, Comet Chaser is bringing Blitzball to students throughout Equestria. Tryouts for his team will be this Friday after school. I hope you're as excited about a Canterlot High Blitzball team as I am."

Rainbow Dash stood up. "Wait…am I dreaming? Did she just say what I think she said?"

"Comet Chaser is coming to our school!" Twilight repeated. "He's starting a program to create a Blitzball high school league!"

"Comet, *the head coach of the Beehive Blitzers*? The first Blitzball player to win MVP in the league?" Rainbow Dash said. "The reason the Blitzers won this season? *One of the toughest players the sport has ever known?*"

"That's him...." Twilight Sparkle smiled.

"You have to try out!" Sunset Shimmer added.

Rainbow Dash couldn't believe it. Comet was a Blitzball legend. Sure, he hadn't played the game in more than a decade, but everyone who knew Blitzball knew his name.

Rainbow Dash grabbed Twilight's hands. She thought she might scream. The only thing better than watching Blitzball would be playing it. For once, she'd have a chance to be part of the action, zipping down the field with the ball, dodging other players as they tried to snatch it from her. She'd have a uniform with her name on the back, with her very own number. Crowds would be cheering, *"Dash! Dash! Rainbow Dash!"*

She straightened up, suddenly serious.

"What's wrong?" Sunset Shimmer asked.

"Friday is only four days away," Rainbow Dash said. "Let's go—I need to practice!"

She grabbed Twilight's and Sunset's hands and they sprinted out of class just as the bell rang. They ran down the hall, heading toward the field.